This Book Belongs To:

KiKi

JE

Praise for *No Biggy!*

"This book gives both young kids and their parents
a fantastic tool to break the cycle of frustration—and better yet,
it does it in the form of a sweet story."

—Cara Natterson, MD,
mother and author, *The Care and Keeping of You*

"*No Biggy!* is the best book I have read that teaches kids the importance
of 'not sweating the small stuff.' It makes a very grown-up lesson easy for kids
to understand and embrace. I definitely recommend it to all parents!"

—Jaime Pressly, mother and Emmy Award-winning actress, *My Name is Earl*

"In a child's world where frustration occurs all the time,
Elycia elegantly and touchingly reminds us that it really is No Biggy!"

—Jeremy F. Shapiro, MD,
father and partner, Boulevard Pediatrics Medical Group, Inc.

"*No Biggy!* is going on our coffee table. EVERYONE should read this wisdom."

—Megyn Price, mother and actress, *Rules of Engagement*

"This delightful book has a great message. The illustrations and facial
expressions are fantastic for teaching children social cues. *No Biggy!* can be a
very useful and fun tool in helping children deal with frustration."

—Penni Seller, PsyD, LMFT,
mother, and child development/parent education specialist

"*No Biggy!* is a hit in our family. We love this book.
It's now become my son's favorite phrase!"

—Sarah Shahi, mother and actress, *Person of Interest*

NO BiGGY!

A Story About Overcoming Everyday Obstacles

Words by Elycia Rubin   Pictures by Josh Talbot

RODALE
KiDS

Lots of things make me feel happy, like playing fetch with my dog, Pozey. Her soft, fuzzy face always makes me smile.

I also love to paint, practice handstands, and eat ice cream.

Sometimes I dream about eating ice cream all day.

Boy, that would be fun!

Lots of things make me feel frustrated too.

Frustrated is a big word I learned from my mommy and daddy.

COME IN, KIKI!

I get **frustrated** in the morning when I squeeze toothpaste on my toothbrush and when I'm about to brush my teeth the toothpaste falls off and goes kerplunk! on the floor.

Sometimes I cry and yell, "Momeeeeeee!" She runs in and says, "No biggy, Kiki. Let's wipe it up and try again."

So I keep trying and trying.

School mornings are nutty. **So many things to do** before the bus arrives!

Getting dressed for school all by myself makes me feel proud, but sometimes I can't get the zipper to slide up my jacket. I get so frustrated I yank it off, throw it on the floor, and huff and puff.

My daddy comes in my room and says, "No biggy. What do you think? Want to try it again?"

I do and I finally get the zipper to go up, and that makes me feel better.

It's fun to help make my breakfast. Sometimes the cream cheese clumps up on my bagel because I'm still practicing how to spread it. I clench my fists and make a noise my mommy and daddy call a grunt.

They look at me and say, "No biggy. Want to try again?"

I practice some more and make a happy face in the cream cheese.

That makes me giggle.

At school we all love building big structures with lots of rainbow tiles. Alex tries to make a diamond shape **but the pieces won't stay together.**

He makes a frustrated face and breaks them apart.

I look at Alex, I look at the pile, and I think. "No biggy," I say. "Maybe we could make something together?"

We work as a team and build a giant diamond and a star.

Alex is so proud and shouts, "Look what we made!"
That makes us both feel really happy.

During story time my teacher says it's my turn to pick a book. I pull out my favorite and get so excited that I rip a page by accident.

All I hear are a bunch of loud "Uh-ohs" from my friends.

I grab the tape. "There, no biggy! All fixed," I blurt out. My teacher smiles and says, "Thank you. That's right, Kiki. What a great lesson—no biggy."

All of my friends start clapping

and I feel so special.

After school, chasing Pozey always makes me laugh. I love watching her big floppy ears bounce up and down. When we go inside she gets mud all over!

My mommy makes a mad face and says,

"Oh no, Pozey is getting dirt everywhere!"

I grab a towel and rub Pozey's paws super clean.

"No biggy, Mommy," I say. She stops and looks at me.

"You're so right, Kiki.

No biggy!"

Taking a bath before bed with lots of orange smelling bubbles is one of my favorite things. When I check the water, I yell, **"Oh no!"** Daddy and Mommy run in.

They both start shouting,

"Oh no, oh nooooo!"

I grab my daddy's giant robe and throw it down. **"There, no biggy!"** I say. My mommy and daddy look at each other.

With the biggest smiles and most proud faces they say,
"Thank you for teaching us this is no biggy!"

Then they tickle me
all over and we just laugh
and laugh and laugh . . .

For our beautiful inside and out Kayla Ever, who inspired this book.
Thank you for always teaching us the most meaningful lessons every single day—
love, kindness, patience, and remembering to take deep breaths. We love you to infinity and beyond!
—E.R.

To my dear little family—Jennifer, Eden, and baby-to-be.
Thank you for reminding me of what is most important in life
and that everything else really is "no biggy."
—J.T.

ACKNOWLEDGMENTS FROM THE AUTHOR

Much gratitude and appreciation for Eric Wight and Anna Cooperberg—
thank you for your patience, support, and guidance. To Brandon Waltman and Dena Verdesca,
thank you for your creativity. To my husband, Brad Kaplan, for being a solid rock (with the best arms!).
And, to my fierce mom, Andrea, whose strength is the greatest inspiration.

RODALE
KiDS

An imprint of Rodale Books
733 Third Avenue
New York, NY 10017
Visit us online at rodalekids.com

Text © 2018 by Elycia Rubin
Illustrations © 2018 by Josh Talbot

Rodale Kids books may be purchased for business or promotional use or for special sales.
For information, please e-mail: RodaleKids@Rodale.com

Printed in China
Manufactured by RRD Asia 201709

Design by Tom Daly

Library of Congress Cataloging-in-Publication Data is on file with the publisher.

ISBN 978–1–63565-048-8 hardcover

Distributed to the trade by Macmillan

10 9 8 7 6 5 4 3 2 1 hardcover